SUPER DC HEROES

BATMAN

ROBIN'S FIRST FLIGHT

WRITTEN BY
ROBERT GREENBERGER

ILLUSTRATED BY
GREGG SCHIGIEL AND
LEE LOUGHRIDGE

BATMAN CREATED BY
BOB KANE

STONE ARCH BOOKS
a capstone imprint

Published by Stone Arch Books in 2010
A Capstone Imprint
151 Good Counsel Drive, P.O. Box 669
Mankato, Minnesota 56002
www.capstonepub.com

Library of Congress Cataloging-in-Publication Data

Greenberger, Robert.
  Robin's first flight / by Robert Greenberger ; illustrated by Gregg Schigiel ;
illustrated by Lee Loughridge.
    p. cm. -- (DC super heroes. Batman)
  ISBN 978-1-4342-1879-7 (library binding) -- ISBN 978-1-4342-2262-6 (pbk.)
  [1. Superheroes--Fiction.] I. Schigiel, Gregg, ill. II. Loughridge, Lee, ill. III.
Title.
  PZ7.G82764Ro 2010
  [Fic]--dc22
                                            2009029089

Summary: Junior high school student Tim Drake is tired of being a hero-in-
training. He's ready to become the full-time sidekick of Batman, Gotham's
Greatest Crime Fighter. The Dark Knight, however, has one final test for his
anxious apprentice, and it won't be easy. Tim will need the help of Nightwing,
Batman's former partner, to complete the timely task and become the next
Robin.

Art Director: Bob Lentz
Designer: Brann Garvey
Production Specialist: Michelle Biedscheid

Printed in the United States of America in Stevens Point, Wisconsin.
032011
006120R

TABLE of CONTENTS

CHAPTER 1

A FINAL TEST

Tim Drake was excited. As he adjusted the mask on his face, he stood in the Batcave, feeling ready to take on the world.

For the last six months, he had been training his mind and body to become the next ally in Batman's fight against crime.

"When do we go on patrol?" the teen asked his mentor.

Batman did not answer. He was adding fresh supplies from a metal cabinet to his Utility Belt.

From the back, the cloaked super hero seemed ominous, even scary, as he stood in the caverns beneath Wayne Manor.

"Well?" prodded Tim.

"You completed your training with the best teachers I could find," Batman said. His voice echoed off the rocky walls. "But that doesn't mean I think you're ready."

"What will convince you?" Tim asked.

"A final test," Batman replied.

"Okay," Tim said. "What do you have in mind?"

Finished with his task, the Dark Knight slowly turned around. The expression under his cowl was unreadable.

"Hide and seek," Batman said.

Tim's jaw dropped open in surprise.

"A kid's game?" Tim asked.

"Not quite," Batman said. "I will be hiding somewhere within Gotham City. There will be one clue at the starting point, and you will have until midnight to find me."

Tim started to protest, but Batman held up his hand. "After all, it's a school night," said the Dark Knight.

Tim shuffled his feet. This wasn't what he expected after months of mastering martial arts, forensics, and science, all while still attending junior high school.

"Fine," he agreed. "When do we begin?"

"Right now," Batman said. "And your chaperone has just arrived."

Tim's eyes narrowed. "I need a babysitter?" he asked. "Who is it? Alfred?"

Batman shook his head. A figure appeared from the shadows, dressed in blue and black, his outfit inspired by Batman's own suit. Tim was surprised to see Dick Grayson, the crime fighter known as Nightwing. He had been the first Robin.

"Hey, Tim," Nightwing said, breaking into a grin. "This should be fun."

"Maybe for you," Tim said.

CHAPTER 2

BAT-SIGNAL BEGINNINGS

While Batman drove the Batmobile
into the city, Tim sat in the passenger seat.
He was ready. He was confident. He knew
he would always honor the uniform. Did
he really need this final test? Well, if it
meant only one more night before officially
becoming Robin, then he figured he could
get through it!

The sleek, dark vehicle parked in an
alley near police headquarters. Batman
leaped out of the car. "Wait five minutes,"
he said. "Then check the roof."

The Dark Knight soared away, his cape fluttering in the evening breeze.

As Tim watched Batman vanish from sight, he heard a sound and looked up. Nightwing was waiting for him on a fire escape. He had a big grin on his face.

"What's so funny?" Tim asked in an irritated voice.

"When he tested me," Nightwing said, "I was just as anxious as you are now."

"Really?" Tim asked.

Nightwing nodded. Then, he crouched and expertly launched himself across the alley to a narrow windowsill. Tim broke into a smile of his own. He leaped from the street and grabbed the ladder of the fire escape. Quickly, he made his way up to where Nightwing was waiting for him.

"So," the older of the two began, "where did Batman hide the clue?"

Tim jerked a thumb over his shoulder at the next building. "Police Headquarters," explained Tim. "Batman said the clue would be on the roof."

Tim positioned himself on a railing of the fire escape. He threw his Batarang up toward the police building's flagpole.

CLINK The Batarang and its rope coiled around the base of the pole. Tim tugged the rope once to test its strength, and then launched himself into the air.

Tim enjoyed the warm breeze that rushed against his face as he swung over the alley and toward the roof.

As he landed on the rooftop, he heard Nightwing touch down beside him.

Sure enough, placed directly atop the unlit Bat-Signal was the clue. It was a playing card — the ace of diamonds.

Tim walked over and examined it without touching the card. Nightwing followed, watching in silence.

Tim took a special light from his belt and shined it on the card. He clicked it off and looked over at Nightwing. "Looks new," he said. "No fingerprints or identifying marks, of course."

"A playing card could mean the Joker," Tim said, thinking aloud. "But I doubt we're going after him as part of the test. The card has to mean something else."

Tim's eyes scanned the rooftop. In the southwest corner, he spotted a single footprint in the dirt and dust.

"Which way, kid?" Nightwing asked.

"Toward the Hill," Tim said, referring to a particularly dangerous part of the city. "The footprint points in that direction."

"What about the playing card?" questioned Nightwing.

"I still need some time to think about that," Tim said. He threw his Batarang into the air. Nightwing followed suit.

Tim crouched on the edge of the roof, ready to swing away, but Nightwing grabbed his arm and pointed. The teen looked and saw a cluster of people standing on a corner less than a block away.

"Got it," Tim said.

The pair of heroes swung toward the people, away from the direction of the Hill.

A moment later, they landed on the street and released their ropes.

Three men in leather jackets were robbing an elderly couple, who cowered in fear. Nightwing crept up behind them and tapped one thug on the shoulder. As the thief turned, a fist met his jaw. WHAM!

Tim tackled another mugger, knocking him to the ground. THUD! With calm, practiced ease, he whipped out a pair of plastic handcuffs from his Utility Belt and secured the man's wrists. CLICK!

Suddenly, the last remaining thug charged at Nightwing with his fist raised.

Tim quickly sprang to his feet and pulled a Batarang out from his Utility Belt. Then he tossed the Batarang at the attacking thief's arm.

Nightwing quickly tackled the thief, subduing him. He looked up at Tim, and said, "Nice one, kid."

Tim beamed with pride.

"Thank you so much," the woman said in a weak voice. "You two are almost as good as Batman!" added her husband.

"Almost," said Nightwing, grinning.

Tim radioed the police and then turned to his partner. "It's getting late," he said. "We need to keep moving."

Nightwing nodded, and once more they were on their way to the Hill.

"Well, it wasn't exactly taking down Two-Face, but I'm glad we could help," Tim said.

"Crime is crime," said Nightwing.

Nightwing's smile suddenly froze as
he looked into the distance. Tim followed
his gaze and saw blinking lights from two
cars that had smashed into one another.
Nightwing shot Tim a glance.

"I know, I know," Tim grumbled. "We
have to make another detour."

They rushed to the scene of the accident
and surveyed the damage. One of the
drivers had gotten out and seemed dazed.
In the other more seriously damaged car, a
woman was trapped.

Tim rushed to the side of the car. The
metal door had been twisted and it could
not be opened. The woman watched with
wide eyes as Tim leaped onto the hood. Tim
gestured for her to remain calm. He pulled
out a device from his Utility Belt and aimed
it at the windshield. *BZZT!*

The device shot out a bright red laser beam. Swiftly, Tim cut around the windshield and tossed it aside.

Once there was an opening, Tim eased into the car and used the laser to puncture the airbag. By then, Nightwing had moved to the hood. He helped his young ally pull the thankful woman to freedom.

Sirens in the distance told them help was on the way.

CHAPTER 3

LEARNING TO ADAPT

As the paramedics tended to the crash victims, Tim and Nightwing continued their way toward the Hill.

"It's already after ten," Tim complained.

"Would you rather have left that woman in the car?" Nightwing asked, as they ran along the rooftops above the city.

"Of course not," Tim replied.

Tim turned his mind back to the playing card that Batman had left. He wondered if a card factory was located in the Hill.

"Our job isn't just about arresting super-villains," Nightwing continued.

"I know, it's just — it's my first night, and I want it to count," Tim said. "I want to find Batman and earn his approval."

"When Batman tested me, I was just as excited as you are," Nightwing said. "But you have to be patient and learn to adapt when things don't go as planned."

Tim looked up at Nightwing and nodded. He knew Dick's advice was good. Nightwing knew more than most people about things going bad.

Tim remembered that Dick Grayson had once been a member of the famous Flying Graysons circus troupe. While performing in Gotham, his parents had fallen to their deaths.

Their trapeze ropes had been cut by criminals who were trying to scare the circus owner into giving them money.

Bruce Wayne had been at the circus that day. As Batman, he comforted the weeping eight-year-old. Having been an orphan of crime himself, Batman took the boy into his home and raised him as his own son.

Years later, Dick had begged Batman for a chance at finding the criminal boss who had caused his parents to be killed. Batman knew that Dick was strong and athletic, so he agreed.

Batman gave Dick a colorful uniform, naming him Robin. The duo eventually tracked down and arrested the criminal who was responsible. It was only afterward that Dick had begun the rest of his training as a crime fighter.

Tim Drake had been lucky. His parents were still alive when they had taken him to see the Graysons perform on that fateful night. Later in life, he saw Robin performing a stunt that the acrobatic family had once done. It was then that Tim figured out Dick Grayson was Robin.

Dick eventually grew up and became Nightwing, leaving Batman to fight crime on his own. Tim was convinced that Batman needed a new partner — a second Robin. He proved he was worthy by revealing the secrets he solved to Batman, who was impressed. Dick gave Tim his approval, which helped decide the matter.

To become the new Robin, Tim had to accept six long months of difficult training. He was schooled in gymnastics, martial arts, escapology, and forensics.

Tim's training had been intense, but the young crime fighter had been up to the task. Stealing time to secretly train with Batman had been easy, too, since Tim's parents were constantly traveling.

However, while Tim's parents had been away on business, a villain called the Obeah Man kidnapped the couple for ransom. Batman rushed to the Caribbean to save them, but he was too late. Tim's mother had died. He did manage to rescue his dad, Jack, who had been injured.

Now, Tim was caring for his father, who was undergoing physical therapy. Between helping his father and secretly training with Batman, Tim had almost no free time.

Fortunately, the Drake home was near Wayne Manor, so visiting the Batcave had been easy enough.

Tim had trained hard. He was ready. All he had to do now was find Batman within the next hour to become the new Robin.

CRASH!! A noise interrupted Tim's thoughts. He swiveled his head around, searching for the source. There, in a park's playground, a gang fight had begun.

"Nightwing!" he called.

"I see it," his partner said.

The two leaped to a nearby rooftop and observed the scene. Tim counted the number of fighters.

"There are a dozen of them," he said.

"Good, six for each of us!" Nightwing said, ready for some action.

Tim nodded, and the two heroes leaped into yet another necessary distraction.

CHAPTER 4

NECESSARY DISTRACTIONS

The gang members, one group dressed in red and the other in green, were so busy fighting with each other that no one noticed the costumed heroes.

Nightwing grabbed one gang member by his leather jacket and pulled him away from the others. "Don't you know the noise is keeping the neighbors up?" he asked with a smirk.

The teen tried to land a punch, but Nightwing was faster. He caught the thug's fist in his open hand. **WHAM!**

"I think you've had enough fun for tonight," Nightwing added. He picked up the thug and tossed him into some bushes.

Tim laughed and then threw himself into the middle of the brawl. Crouching low, he spun in a circle next to the gangsters. He used his left leg to sweep their feet, tripping several fighters to the ground.

He and Nightwing quickly separated the gangsters, removing their weapons one by one. Suddenly disarmed, the two groups just stood there, breathing heavily, staring at the masked duo.

"We could keep this up all night," Nightwing said. "But, you guys can't. You're sloppy and undisciplined."

"This isn't your fight," said one of the teens. He wore a red bandana.

"True," Tim agreed. "But now it's no one's fight. This is about turf, right? The Red Fists want control of the park, which the Green Flames have claimed for years."

One gangster, and then another, nodded in agreement.

"Your leaders need to settle this dispute and keep the peace," Tim continued. "Or we will be back."

"That's it? You're leaving us?" one teen asked.

Tim walked closer, and the guy took a step backward. "The police have already been called by the neighbors watching from the apartments," Tim said. "Start fighting again, and all of you will get arrested. Now get out of here and call it a night."

The teens drifted away, one by one.

"Good work," Nightwing said, placing a hand on Tim's shoulder.

"Thanks, but now it's after eleven o'clock," replied Tim. "We have to get a move on if I have any chance of finding Batman."

He turned to leave, but then paused when he heard a soft sound. Someone was crying, and it wasn't a gang member.

Carefully, he walked toward a cluster of trees in the corner of the park. As Tim neared them, he slowed down. He saw a whimpering young child.

"It's okay. I'm a friend," Tim said softly.

The young girl was hiding between a tree and a chain-link fence. She had been crying for quite some time. She was shivering in the cold night air.

"What's your name?" asked Tim.

"Elizabeth," she said between sobs.

"Are you lost?" Tim asked.

"Yes," Elizabeth said, sniffling.

"I can help you," Tim said. He extended one hand toward her. She considered it for a moment, staring at his black mask. Then she met his hand with her own.

The two walked away from the trees toward the better-lit central area of the park. Nightwing stood there, returning his radio to his side.

"I've already called the police to help find her parents," he said.

"Thanks," Tim said, squeezing the girl's hand. She had stopped crying and was now staring at Nightwing in awe.

"Are you Batman?" the girl asked Nightwing. "Where's your cape?"

Tim chuckled. "No, that's his friend Nightwing," Robin said. "Batman's missing, and we're looking for him."

"He's lost like me?" she asked.

"Not quite," Tim said. "More like hiding."

"You better find him," Elizabeth said. "Mom says we need him."

"Very true," Tim said.

It took a few minutes before the police arrived. It was nearly midnight. Tim hid his concern about the time from the girl.

Instead, Tim asked Elizabeth about where her parents lived, to make it easier for the police to bring her home.

A uniformed officer arrived shortly after. Tim told the officer everything the little girl had told him about her home and her parents. The officer led Elizabeth away while Tim waved good-bye.

Once they had left, Tim turned to Nightwing. The older hero was listening to his radio with a frown on his face.

"Now what?" asked Tim.

"A jewelry store alarm just sounded about eight blocks from here," said Nightwing. "It sounds like a break-in."

Tim sighed and said, "I know. I know. We have to go help."

CHAPTER 5

FINDING THE JEWEL THIEF

The young heroes seemed to be in a friendly race to beat each other to the jewelry store. Soon, Tim and Nightwing were standing side by side, looking down at the streets from a rooftop.

Tim didn't hear any sirens from the top of the building. He suspected the police were still busy dealing with the gangs and the lost girl.

"Looks like it's just us," Tim said.

"What do you see?" Nightwing asked.

"The jewel thieves must have entered through the rear door," Tim explained. "No lookouts. No getaway car. They must be hoping to grab the jewels and just walk away."

"Sounds about right," Nightwing agreed. "What do we do?"

"Wait for them to come out rather than trash the store," Tim said with confidence.

"Let's get in position," Nightwing said. He ran along the rooftop to reach a spot above the rear entrance of the jewelry store. Tim followed, feeling better about the situation.

As the two watched and waited, a large shadow appeared in the doorway.

Without hesitation, Tim launched himself off the rooftop.

Tim rappelled down the building with practiced ease. Halfway to the ground, he kicked hard off the concrete wall and flipped backward, releasing the rope.

Tim landed a few feet from the thief. He stood in front of the masked man.

"You can drop the jewels and let me cuff you," Tim suggested. "Or you can fight — and lose."

The man was tall and broad. He was wearing a black trench coat and a ski mask. His gloved hand stuffed a bag into his coat's deep pocket.

When his hand came back out, it was holding a long, glimmering knife. He crouched and then lunged forward. His knife was pointed directly at Tim.

"Fight it is," Tim said, flexing his legs.

Tim flipped backward. **THWACK!** His feet kicked the knife out of the man's hand. As Tim landed, the unarmed criminal rushed him again. The man wrapped his bulky arms around Tim. The teen was trapped in a bear hug. The man squeezed with surprising strength. Tim couldn't breathe, and his sides began to hurt.

THUD! Tim stomped his right boot heel into the attacker's foot. The man's grip loosened. Tim crouched, slipping from his arms. Then Tim sprang up and rammed his head into the thief's jaw. That sent the man falling backward. Tim stood with his arms crossed, standing over the man.

He broke into a smile, and said, "Game's over, Bruce. I've found you." With that, the boy reached out and pulled off the mask, revealing the face of Bruce Wayne.

"When did you figure it out?" Bruce asked.

"Well, let's start with your general build. You made no attempt to hide that," Tim said. "Then there was the fact that you were doing this entirely by foot late at night without a crowd to hide in. Then, when I attacked you, two things happened. Nightwing stayed back, even though earlier tonight he helped me take down some criminals. Then there was the fact that you didn't even try to punch me — you didn't want to hurt your star pupil."

"Anything else?" Bruce asked.

Tim thought for a moment. "Yeah," he said. "You pulled out a knife when most crooks would have used a gun. Batman never uses a gun, even when playing hide and seek."

"And?" asked Batman, staring at him.

Tim blinked uncertainly.

Nightwing cleared his throat to attract Tim's attention. He pointed to the name on the sign above them: Ace Jewelry Store.

The teen's eyes widened under his mask.

"Of course!" Tim exclaimed. "The ace of diamonds — the first clue."

By now, Batman was back on his feet. He was relocking the door to the store.

"You pointed me in this direction," Tim continued, "but I kept getting distracted."

Batman gave him a puzzled look, so Tim recounted all the times he and Nightwing had to take detours.

Nightwing added, "Tim never rushed in foolishly. He was always patient."

Nightwing continued, "He studied the situation and determined what needed to be done. He looked for clues. He tried to resolve a fight through words, not fists. Pretty good work for his first night."

When Nightwing had finished, Batman nodded and cracked a rare smile.

"Then tonight you learned the most valuable lesson," Bruce said.

Tim nodded slowly. "We have to protect everyone," Tim said.

"Right," said Batman. "The police are good at what they do, but even they have their limits. Whenever possible, we support their efforts to keep Gotham safe."

Nightwing walked over to Tim and ruffled his hair. "I was a lot like you when I first started out," he explained.

Nightwing added, "I thought every night would be spent chasing Catwoman and the Joker — nothing else. But sometimes it's more rewarding to help a lost child."

"You've learned a lot tonight," Batman said. He opened his trench coat to reveal his Batsuit underneath. Placing the cowl over his face, Bruce Wayne was once more the Dark Knight. "You showed compassion, you were calm under pressure, and you studied the facts before acting. You've learned your lessons well."

"Now?" Tim asked eagerly.

"Now you can go on active duty . . . Robin," Batman said to his new partner.

"Yes!" Tim exclaimed.

"My work here is done," Nightwing said. "You'll make a great replacement, Robin."

Nightwing and Batman shook hands. Then Nightwing jumped, grabbed a window ledge, climbed to the rooftops, and vanished from sight.

Moments later, two arms shot their grapnel guns into the sky. A pair of dark figures took flight above the streets, ready to protect Gotham City together.

Nightwing

REAL NAME: Dick Grayson
OCCUPATION: Policeman, Crime Fighter
BASE: Bludhaven

HEIGHT:
5 feet 10 inches

WEIGHT:
175 pounds

EYES:
Blue

HAIR:
Black

Dick Grayson was a member of the Flying Graysons, a family of circus acrobats. After Dick's parents were murdered, Bruce Wayne adopted the troubled youth. Grayson was determined to catch the criminals who had killed his parents, and he asked Batman to train him to become a super hero. Dick showed a lot of talent in his training, impressing the Dark Knight. Soon, Batman made Grayson the first Robin, and the two paired up to fight crime. Later, Dick made his own super hero costume by adding touches to Batman's suit. Nightwing was born.

Robin

REAL NAME: Tim Drake

OCCUPATION: Student, Crime Fighter

BASE: Gotham City

HEIGHT:
5 feet 1 inch

WEIGHT:
115 pounds

EYES:
Blue

HAIR:
Black

Tim got his chance to become the next Robin when Dick Grayson, the previous Robin, became Nightwing. Tim, quite brilliant for his age, discovered the secret identities of Nightwing *and* Batman. The teen approached Grayson and shared his discovery, impressing him. With Dick's approval, Batman accepted Tim into the Bat family and gave him the Robin mantle. As the current Robin, Tim Drake soars alongside Batman as one half of the Dynamic Duo, fighting against the criminal elements of Gotham City.

BIOGRAPHIES

Robert Greenberger began his career at *Starlog Press*. He then joined DC Comics as an assistant editor and eventually became Manager of Editorial Operations. In 2001, he became Marvel's Director of Publishing Operations. In 2002, he went back to DC Comics as a Senior Editor in its collected editions department. Bob then joined *Weekly World News* as Managing Editor until its end in 2007. Since then, he has been a full-time freelance writer and editor. Bob has written many short works of fiction, including *The Essential Batman Encyclopedia* and *Batman Vault*. Bob lives in Fairfield, Connecticut, with his wife, Deb, and their dog, Dixie.

Gregg Schigiel is originally from South Florida. He has wanted to be a cartoonist since he was 11 years old. Gregg has worked on projects featuring Batman, Spider-Man, SpongeBob SquarePants, and just about everything in between. Gregg currently lives and works in New York City.

Lee Loughridge has been working in comics for more than 14 years. He currently lives in sunny California in a tent on the beach.

GLOSSARY

acrobatic (ak-ruh-BAT-ik)—difficult gymnastic movement usually done in the air

adapt (uh-DAPT)—to change because of a new situation or experience

adjusted (uh-JUHST-id)—moved or changed something slightly

anxious (ANGK-shuss)—very eager and nervous

compassion (kuhm-PASH-uhn)—a feeling of sympathy for someone

cowered (KOU-urd)—to crouch in fear or shame

deduced (di-DOOSSD)—figured something out from clues or from what you already know

ominous (OM-uh-nuhss)—a feeling that something bad is going to happen

resolve (ri-ZOLV)—to deal with a problem or situation successfully

subduing (suhb-DOO-ing)—defeating someone in battle, or calming and controlling something

DISCUSSION QUESTIONS

1. Which is more important — protecting the innocent, or catching criminals? Why?

2. Nightwing, Robin, and Batman each have unique costumes and personalities. If you could be a super hero, which one would you want to be like?

3. Robin and Nightwing help a lost child. Have you ever helped someone? Talk about it.

WRITING PROMPTS

1. More than anything, Robin wants to be respected and treated like an adult. Have you ever felt like you were being treated like a child? How did it make you feel? Write about it.

2. Write another chapter to this book where Robin takes flight on his own to fight crime. What kinds of criminals does he catch? What super-villain does he fight? You decide.

3. Robin has to go through intense training to become a super hero. Have you ever had to do something difficult? Write about your experience.

MORE NEW BATMAN ADVENTURES!

KILLER CROC HUNTER

TWO-FACE'S
DOUBLE TAKE

BAT-MITE'S
BIG BLUNDER

CATWOMAN'S
CLASSROOM OF CLAWS

ARCTIC ATTACK